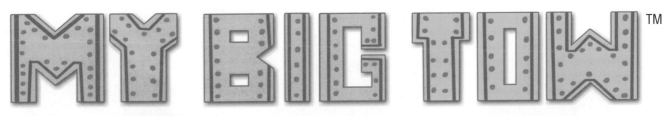

MY BIG TOW™
THE ADVENTURES OF CAPTAIN RECOVERY™

Written by Kyle Chirgwin

Illustrated by Joshua Otero

D1294868

Darren and his little sister Kaylee
are playing in their backyard sandbox.

Darren plays with the toy trucks.

He picks up his favorite blue tow truck and his
imagination takes over. Suddenly Darren, a five-year old boy,
turns into Captain Recovery – known for all the big recovery jobs
he does with Big Blue, a shiny new heavy-duty tow truck.

4

As the phone rings early in the morning, Captain Recovery picks up the receiver. It's a big tow job. The adventure begins...

This job is going to be very hard.

At the airport, a jetliner slid off the end of the runway.

Captain Recovery arrives at the shop, opens the big bay door and starts up Big Blue.

Kody, one of the shop dogs, pants, ready to go for another ride.

6

After a few minutes, Big Blue is warmed up,
aired up and ready to go.

Captain Recovery puts Kody in the cab
and heads to the airport.

Kody sits in the front, looking all around.
Along the way, Captain Recovery wonders
what he's going to be up against.

How far is the plane off the runway?
Are the tires still inflated?
Is it stuck in mud because it rained yesterday?

7

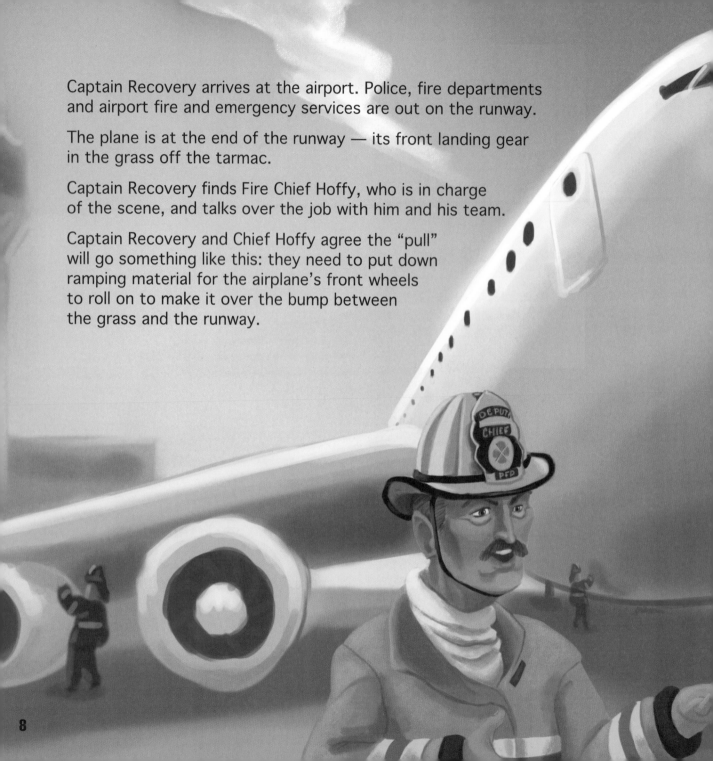

Captain Recovery arrives at the airport. Police, fire departments and airport fire and emergency services are out on the runway.

The plane is at the end of the runway — its front landing gear in the grass off the tarmac.

Captain Recovery finds Fire Chief Hoffy, who is in charge of the scene, and talks over the job with him and his team.

Captain Recovery and Chief Hoffy agree the "pull" will go something like this: they need to put down ramping material for the airplane's front wheels to roll on to make it over the bump between the grass and the runway.

Captain Recovery jumps back into Big Blue and gives Kody a pat on the head. Kody lets out a friendly bark.

Captain Recovery positions Big Blue, takes out all of the big straps he needs, and rigs up the gear.

When the rigging is done, Captain Recovery pulls out the cables from the two big winches and hooks them to the straps.

After checking with Fire Chief Hoffy to make sure all is well and the ramping is in place, Captain Recovery works the tow truck's levers and the winches slowly pull the plane back onto the runway.

After pulling the airplane about 25 feet, it is safely on the tarmac.

Captain Recovery packs up his gear and places it back into Big Blue.

He pulls in the cables and brings in the boom, then finishes up the paperwork and says goodbye to Fire Chief Hoffy.

14

Kody is barking up a storm in the cab of the truck. Captain Recovery walks over to see what the fuss is about.

Someone was talking over the "squawk box."

"This is Kaylee at base. We have another big job this afternoon at the rail yard. Better head on in."

Woof ... woof! Captain Recovery could hear their other shop dog Balto in the background. Balto is a black lab that likes to stay with Kaylee and Auntie Lisa at the shop office.

Suddenly, at high noon, Auntie Lisa calls everyone in for lunch.

As Darren lines up his trucks in the sandbox, he parks Big Blue in its spot and calls for Kody and Balto to come into the house with him.

Darren can hardly wait until after lunch to get back into the sandbox and take Big Blue on the next big job for Captain Recovery!